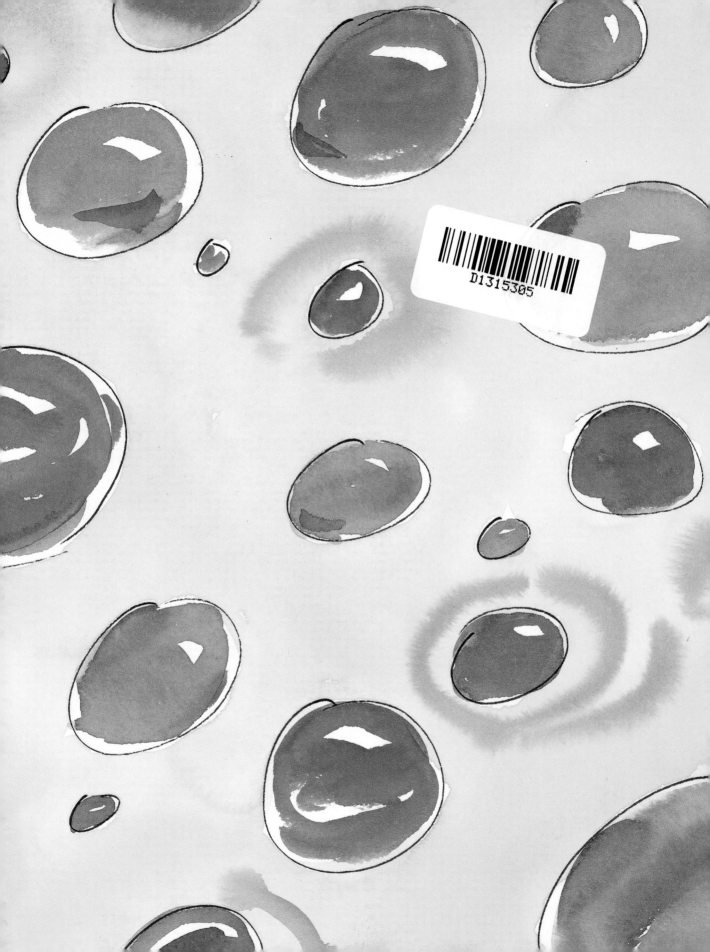

CYNTHIA DeFELICE

Casey
in the
Bath

Pictures by Chris L. Demarest

Farrar Straus Giroux
New York

For Mac,
who sang to me in the tub
—C.C.D.

Library of Congress Cataloging-in-Publication Data. DeFelice, Cynthia C. Casey in the bath / Cynthia DeFelice : illustrated by Chris L. Demarest. — 1st ed.   n I.   [1. Baths—Fiction.]   I. Demarest, Chris L., ill.   II. Title.   PZ7.D3597Cas   1996   [E] — dc20   95-8399 MARC Partial   AC

One summer day there was a knock at the door.
Casey and his mother both went to answer it, and
there, on the porch, stood a strange little man. In his
hand was a large, squashy-looking suitcase.

"Hello," he said, with a grin that made his mustache curl. "I'm your Ambrosial Products representative." He reached into his suitcase, took out a bottle, and held it up. "Could I interest you in some of our amazing new bath soap?"

Casey frowned. "No," he said.

"Well . . ." said Casey's mother.

"It's guaranteed to make taking a bath a *thrilling* experience!" the salesman said, winking at Casey.

"Fat chance," said Casey.

But his mother said, "I'll try anything that might get Casey into the tub." And she bought a bottle.

That night, Casey was watching television. His father said, "Turn off the TV now, Casey. I've got your bath all ready."

"Aw, Dad, do I *have* to?" Casey asked.

Casey's father didn't answer. He just folded his arms across his chest and looked at Casey.

Casey knew that look. He got up and went down the
hallway and into the bathroom. He took off his clothes,
climbed into the tub, and looked around for the soap.
"Guess I'll have to use this new stuff Mom bought today."

Casey squirted three globs of green goo into the
water. Immediately, huge green bubbles began to form.
"Neat!" said Casey. He popped the biggest bubble.
Out came a green creature.

"*Urp lrp lrp brp,*" the creature said, grinning at Casey and pointing to the other bubbles.

"Oh," said Casey. "Okay." And he began popping *all* the bubbles.

Out of each one came another green creature. Some were big. Some were small. Some were girls. Some were boys. They were all friendly, in a gooey sort of way.

They climbed all over Casey as he sat in the tub. They slid down his arms into the water. Then some of the bravest ones climbed way up to the top of his head, dove off, and landed in the water with a tremendous *splash*! The not-so-brave ones got as far as the tip of his nose and dove from there. That tickled.

Then they played hide-and-go-seek. One hid behind Casey's left ear. Another hid between his toes. One hid in his belly button. That *really* tickled.

Just then Casey's mother appeared at the bathroom door.
"Are you still in the tub?" she asked.

All the green creatures quickly swam under Casey's legs.

His mother looked at Casey and her eyes grew wide.
"You washed *everywhere*! That salesman was right. This
stuff is amazing."

Then Casey's mother leaned over the tub. "Now let's get you rinsed off. It's time for bed," she said. And she pulled the plug.

All the bathwater—and all the green creatures—were getting sucked down the drain.

"Wait!" Casey cried. "Don't leave! Will you ever come back?"

"Yrp urp lrp," answered the creatures, pointing at the bottle. Grinning and waving, they slid down the drain.

Casey's mother was looking at him strangely. "What are you talking about, honey?" she said. "I'm not going anywhere."

"Never mind, Mom," said Casey. "Can I take a bath again tomorrow night?"

The next night, Casey squirted three globs of green
goo into the water. Big green bubbles started to form
again, and Casey began popping.
   "Hi, guys!"
   "Hlrp nrp prp!"

They played Capture the Flag and King on the Mountain. Casey's washcloth was the flag, and Casey was the mountain.

The next night, Casey brought his Lock-Blocks into the tub. He built towers and castles and ships for his friends to play on.

The night after that, he brought in his entire dinosaur collection, and all the green guys played "cave creatures."

The following night, he brought his cassette player and all his tapes into the bathroom, and everybody boogied in the tub.

But the night after that, the bottle was empty.

In the morning, there was a knock at the door. Casey ran to answer it. It was the Ambrosial Products representative!

"I just happened to be in the neighborhood," he said.

"You have any more of that green stuff?" Casey asked eagerly.

"No," the man answered.

Casey's face fell.

"However . . . could I recommend some of our fantastic new purple toothpaste? It's guaranteed to make brushing your teeth a *thrilling* experience." He winked at Casey.

Casey's mother looked doubtful. "Purple toothpaste?" she said. "I don't know . . ."

But Casey shouted, "We'll take ten!"

He grabbed a tube of toothpaste, ran to the
bathroom, and squirted a long purple blob onto his
brush. Large purple bubbles started to form.

Casey began popping . . .

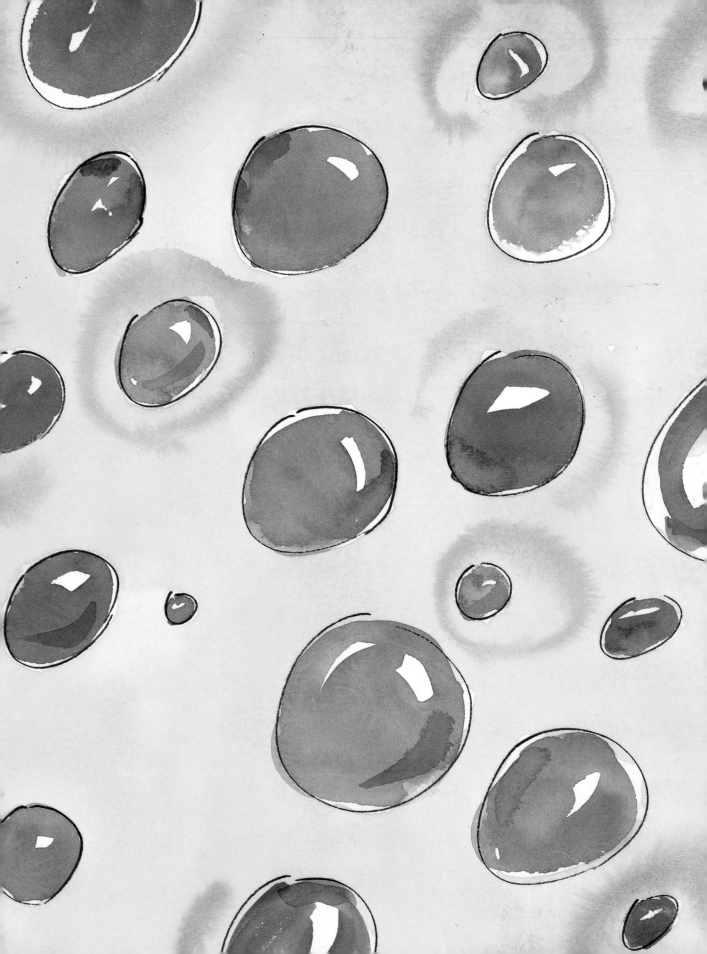